The Sea Piper

The Sea Piper

Helen Cresswell

Illustrated by Jason Cockcroft

Hodder
Children's
Books

a division of Hodder Headline plc

In memory of
the lost children of Aberfan
21st October 1966

Contents

CHAPTER ONE

THE GARTERS

DAVY AND FANCY GARTER WERE shrimpers born and bred. Even their daughter Harriet had been casting her net in pools since she was three years old. They lived close to the sea-shore in a ramshackle old wooden house that shivered and leaned with every wind and yet, for some reason, never blew right away. It was right on the edge of the jetty

where everyday a clockwork tide came
smacking up and then went down again,
leaving the bare, quiet, pool-strewn sand.

The people of Little Shrimpton were
all shrimpers, if it came to that, and the
day the shrimps disappeared seemed like
the end of the world for them.

That day started like any other. Fancy
got up first, as she always did, slamming
the shutters back more to make sure every-
body else woke up than for any other
reason, for it was five o'clock and black as
pitch outside.

Harriet, lying in her narrow trundle
bed, could hear her grumbling and waited
for the moment when the door would
open and the golden shaft of lamplight
would fall across the wall.

One by one she heard the familiar
morning noises, the rattle of the latch,
the working of the old iron pump, the
clatter of pots and pans. Then, in the inter-
vals of silence, she heard the rain, pattering
steadily on the roof and against the walls

and windows of her tiny room.

Harriet decided at once to stay ashore. On fine days she would sometimes go with her father and help with the nets, but a day of dripping oilskins and wet, raw hands and no view through a curtain of rain was not to her taste at all.

The door opened and the knife of lamplight cut across the bed.

"Breakfast," said Fancy, and was gone.

Obediently Harriet swung her legs out of bed and found her clothes in the half darkness. Her room led straight into the living room, and when she went out the table was already set and Davy was laying out his gear.

Out through the scullery she went and into the tiny yard to the pump. The rain beat cold on her bare arms and face, and when she looked up there was not a sign of a star.

She worked the pump noisily to make sure that Fancy heard, gave her face and hands a quick splash and stumbled back inside. Thankfully she shut the door.

"*Wet* again," remarked Fancy. "I sometimes wonder if shrimps is worth all the trouble."

This was a remark she often made and, as she obviously did not mean it, it was always ignored. Shrimps *were* worth the trouble, all the Garters knew that. Fancy, with an iron pot boiling and a basket of wicked-eyed shrimps on her knees ready to be 'got pink', knew it most of all.

"I don't mind a drop of rain," said Davy, drawing up his chair. "It'll be clear by eleven."

"That's what you always say," said Fancy. "As if the *rain* knew what time it was!"

She sat steaming bowls of porridge on the table. As they breakfasted, slowly the grey dawn light filled the windows and the glow of the oil lamp began to pale. Then from the street outside came the tramping of feet on the cobbles and shouts as the fishermen greeted each other on the jetty.

Harriet, wiping the steamy panes, could see their figures outlined against the sky. Behind her Davy was drawing on his rubber leggings and in the scullery Fancy was slapping butter and cheese on bread and packing slab cake in Davy's basket.

"I shan't come to wave you off," said Harriet as Davy straightened up.

"No. Don't you do that. You stop and give your mother a hand," said Davy. He was almost invisible now under his oilskins, but Harriet could see his eyes, bright and excited under the drooping of his sou'wester, and for a moment almost envied him and wished she were going too.

"I'll be there for weighing," she promised.

That was the best moment of all, counting the day's catch on the twilit quay, sniffing the strong wet smell that came up from the dripping nets. It is the only time of the day that a real shrimper ever *can* smell shrimps.

Davy tucked his basket under his arm and was gone. Fancy and Harriet watched him from the door, splashing through the puddles towards the jetty where a full tide was impatiently tossing the boats.

"It'll be a good day," said Fancy closing the door.

That is where she was wrong.

CHAPTER TWO

NO SHRIMPS

HARRIET AND FANCY SPENT THE
morning in the outhouse on the
other side of the yard where
Fancy cleaned and boiled the shrimps. First
there was yesterday's catch for boiling. This
was the part that Fancy loved. To her, a
shrimp was only really a shrimp when it
looked like one – rosy and raw as a newly
bathed baby, pink to its very whiskers. She

crooned as she ladled them from pot to basket.

Afterwards they scoured the big iron pot and made neat stacks of the bowls and baskets that went to market. They had just finished when they heard the wheels rattling over the cobbles and Fancy cried "Horn!" and out they both ran.

"Father was right," said Harriet. "Fine before eleven."

Fancy did not hear. She was jostling her way through the throng that had gathered around Horn's cart. Every day he went to market at Lower Herring down the coast, taking the day's catch for the whole village. Now he was bringing back the empty baskets and, of course, the money.

Horn was a thin, surprised looking man not unlike a shrimp himself. He had a shock of hair that seemed to stand up straight, beady eyes and a very little chin. He was standing on his cart, slate in hand and money-bag to his elbow, calling off

names and making a thorough-going
business of it all. Each wife came forward
as her name was called and collected her
baskets, while Horn counted out the
copper and silver and the rest craned and
peered. When Fancy came back her face
was very red. She opened her hand and
Harriet saw a single gold piece. Only once
or twice a year did gold come back from
the market.

"Gold!" she cried.

Fancy nodded and thrust her hand deep in the pocket of her apron.

"That's for a new chimney when the time for fires comes," she said with satisfaction. The chimney had been threatening to blow off for years, and had finally gone in a spring gale – gone to sea, they supposed, for there was not a trace of it in the morning.

Fancy took the empty baskets back home and stacked them high in good humour.

"And another good day today," she said. "Another gold piece, I shouldn't wonder. It'll be new laced boots for you, Harriet, if it comes off."

This promise sent Harriet earlier than usual to her look-out post on the jetty that evening. She ran out along the black tarry beams of the breakwater to catch up with the tide, which was on its way out for the second time that day. It sucked and hissed on either side and every now and then

managed a little extra slap to splash
Harriet's skirt and stockings. She shaded
her hands over her eyes, because the sails
would come right out of the setting sun
like moths round a candle.

She sighted them at last, gave a warning

cry and ran back along the timbers to stand by the giant scales that stood ready for the weighing. All the wives of the village were out, and Horn himself came down, nodding and bowing as befits a man who hands out silver daily.

Soon the boats were inside the harbour wall and being made fast, and it seemed like any evening out of a thousand other evenings until the first man stepped ashore and without a backward look at his boat walked away. A second man followed, then another. Harriet stared. Davy himself climbed up now and Harriet pulled on Fancy's arm and whispered, "What's the matter? Why doesn't he pull up the net?"

"Hush!" hissed Fancy.

The shrimpers all gathered together and advanced to the enormous iron arms of the scales. The villagers watched. There they stood, fishermen on the one side of the scales, wives on the other. The crying of gulls stopped abruptly – or perhaps it had stopped long ago and nobody had noticed. They stood silent in the creeping dusk and Harriet could not think for the life of her what had happened, what was happening.

"Are we ready for the weighing, then?"

It was Horn, and if he had suddenly given a blast on his horn the effect could not have been greater. Harriet jumped.

"There'll be no weighing," Davy said at last.

"What's that?" cried Horn. "And why not?"

"There'll be no weighing," said Davy, "because there's naught to *be* weighed."

"What?" cried Horn. "*What*?"

A stir ran through the crowd. Davy held up his hand.

"We have sailed all day and cast our nets all day," he said, "and not a man of us has had any luck. There's no shrimps."

"No shrimps!" the exclamation passed among the crowd in an excited hiss. Fancy's skirt jerked suddenly from Harriet's fingers and her wooden shoes clattered over the stones.

"But, Davy," she cried, "the shrimps are *swarming*! See what Horn has brought us from the market!"

She thrust out her hand and the gold gleamed in the cold twilight. Slowly Davy shook his head.

"That was yesterday, Fancy," he said.

"Yesterday! The shrimps have been with us a hundred years! My father was a shrimper, and my grandfather, and my great-grandfather, and my- oh, anyhows, shrimps don't just make off in the night. There's sometimes more and there's sometimes less, that I don't deny, but as to there being none at all...!"

"There's none at all, Fancy," repeated Davy.

They all stood there, nonplussed.

"So we'd best go home and eat our suppers and wait for the morning," he said.

It was the only thing to do. The Garters led the way and they were soon sitting round the table in the lamplit room, where it seemed more impossible than ever that there should be no shrimps.

"You may as well say there's no birds," said Fancy, pouring the gravy. "You may as well say the sea's run dry!"

"The sea might as well have gone dry," said Davy, "if there's no shrimps there."

"They'll be back tomorrow," said
Fancy.

Harriet wondered whether her mother
thought the shrimps had just gone visiting.
On the whole, though, she was taking it
very well. She took out the gold piece
again and smacked it on the table in front
of Davy's plate.

"There goes the chimney," she
remarked. Then, brightening, "Unless you
catch twice the shrimps tomorrow, Davy.
All today's and all tomorrow's! Think of it !
Won't those nets be stuffed? And two gold
pieces when Horn comes from the market.
Chimney and laced boots all at one go.
Fancy that!"

Fancy, in the right mood, could fancy
anything.

After supper she made Davy drag an
old net indoors.

"You might be needing it with all them
shrimps," she said.

The three of them sat round mending
it, seated cross-legged on the rush matting,

while Fancy talked about shrimping in her
father's day, and her grandfather's, and her
great-grandfather's.

"But never before a day without a
single shrimp!" she cried happily. "*This*'ll
be a day to remember, Davy!"

As the wick burned lower their spirits burned higher. When they went to bed it was to dream of shrimps in great, misty shoals, seas full of shrimps, all swimming down the cold tide towards the blossoming nets of Davy Garter. Fancy had won the day.

CHAPTER THREE

DAVY TRIES AGAIN

NEXT MORNING DAVY WENT OFF
as usual with very little said about
the happenings of the day before.
The only difference was that today Harriet
and Fancy went out with him to the jetty
to lend a hand with the mended net.

"There'll be no need for it, Fancy," he
kept protesting. "I've never needed more
nets in my whole life."

"You will today," said Fancy firmly, and the net went with him.

Harriet and Fancy stood and watched the sails dissolve into the mist. It was very still and only a little dawn breeze carried them down the tide.

"Perfect," remarked Fancy. "Absolutely perfect."

For all that she was not in a very good mood that morning. The were no shrimps for boiling, and she prowled restlessly about the house, finding fault with every-thing.

"It's at times like this I could envy your Aunt Lavinia," she told Harriet. Aunt Lavinia was not in fact Harriet's aunt at all, she was Fancy's, a fact which Fancy chose to ignore. "At least she's always got some-thing to put her hand to. *Shells* don't go swimming off in the night."

Aunt Lavinia lived at Lower Herring and made her living by gathering shells and turning them into all kinds of unlikely objects. Two penguins with mussel shells

for wings stood on the dresser as a memento of her last visit, and Harriet herself had
endless coloured cockle necklaces and
painted shell-boxes. There were shells
galore at Lower Herring, at Little
Shrimpton hardly any.

Once the sun was fully up and sprinkling light on the salty flats, Harriet took
her shrimping net and went off. Fancy was
not very good company that morning, and
in any case Harriet herself felt restless and
fidgety. Fancy's dreams of a vast shrimp
harvest had seemed well enough the night
before, but this morning they *were* only
dreams and wanted putting to the test.
Harriet wanted to see a shrimp with her
own eyes. She felt as if it were a hundred
years since she had last seen one.

Barefoot she picked her way over the
stranded purple and green of the seaweed
and with a thumping heart bent over the
first pool. It was clear and shallow, only a
flat puddle really, full of blue sky and with
only a single tiny starfish to show that the

tide had been. She hurried her steps down the beach towards the real pools, the deep ones, where a morning's patience wih her net could fill a basket and earn her a few coppers of her own.

Time and again she drew her net through the water, in the end running from pool to pool until at last, breathless and nearly a mile away from home, she gave up. For a while she sat there, staring at the sea, half expecting it to look different now that the shrimps were gone.

Even then she half-heartedly trailed a few pools on the way home, in the hopes of capturing just an odd one, a lost one or a loiterer.

"If I could find just *one*," she thought. "Where there's one there must be more."

At home she told Fancy, who had washed all the curtains and was now scrubbing the floor. She leaned back on her heels and stared.

"*That's* nothing!" she said at last.

"But not one, Mother, not a single one!" cried Harriet.

"That's one tide," said Fancy. "That's yesterday's tide that left them pools. Your father's gone out on a new tide. Those bits of pools down there don't mean a thing, that I *am* sure of."

Harriet at once saw the truth of this. She put her shrimping net away and began to wonder what was for dinner. Even so, for the rest of the day she kept glancing out over the puddled sands and was grateful when at last the tide turned and began to swallow them, one by one.

The whole village turned out that night. Long before the fleet was sighted they were out on the jetty, filled with the promise of certain excitement. Shrimps or no shrimps, excitement there must be.

When at last the shrimpers did come in from the cold sea to the warm pocket of air within the harbour wall, it was like last night all over again, except that this time there was no need of questions. Even Horn had nothing to say.

Families drifted off home, one by one. The Garters themselves went in and shut the door and sat down to supper in silence. No one felt very much like eating. Fancy had been so sure of nets filled to bursting

that she had made a special treat, a deco-
rated cake such as she usually made only
for a party. Now they sat and looked at it
dolefully, hoping they would find the heart
to try a slice when the time came.

"None at all, Davy?" Fancy asked at
last.

"None at all."

"There could be *three* times as many
tomorrow," she suggested, though without
much enthusiasm.

Davy shook his head.

"They've gone. Clean gone."

"Why have they gone, Father?" asked Harriet.

"That I don't know," he replied.

"There's no reading the mind of a shrimp," remarked Fancy, and the others nodded their heads in agreement. That was certainly true.

"Will you try again tomorrow?" asked Fancy then.

"What else is there to do?" said Davy. "Try and try and try again – that's all there is to do."

Fancy collected the dishes and cut into the cake.

"Drat them shrimps!" she burst out then. "Ruination little things! And you'd think butter wouldn't melt in their mouths to see them come out of the pot. All our lives we've spent on shrimps, and this is how they serve us!"

She served out three enormous slices of cake that the knife had cut while carried away by her feelings. Stolidly the three Garters munched their way through it, as if it were a point of honour that none should be left – and another victory for the shrimps if any were.

Tonight there was no net to mend, and Fancy's fancies ran to gloom.

"We've got a bit put by," she said, "but when that's gone we're ruined."

"Now then, Fancy," said Davy, "don't get black."

"I feel black," she said. "Black, black, black! What are we to do if they don't come back? We shall all end up gluing shells like Aunt Lavinia, I know we shall!"

"Except there aren't no shells," Davy reminded her.

"I don't care if there are or not!" cried Fancy "I ain't spending my life gluing shells and stringing cockles. I was brought up to shrimps, and proud of it, and a shrimper I'll stay!"

"Why then, Fancy, so were all of us," said Davy. "And we shall just have to sit quiet and wait what the tide brings us. And perhaps we shan't have to wait so long, after all."

Now it was Davy's turn to be wrong.

CHAPTER FOUR

DOWN THE COAST

NEXT DAY THE FLEET WENT BRAVELY
out to sea again, and the next.
Each night the villagers, after a
long empty day with no boiling, no Horn
with his silver from Lower Herring, waited
on the jetty. Each night they read the news
on the faces of the shrimpers as soon as
they sailed within the harbour wall.

Two weeks after the shrimps disappeared

they held a meeting. The shrimpers came home early that day and went to put on their best clothes first, feeling that the occasion demanded it. Scrubbed, damp-whiskered and best-booted they gathered by the scales. The tide was right in, as if curiosity had got the better of it, and it nudged up close, determined to hear every word.

Harriet herself kept glancing nervously at it, half wondering if it were eaves-dropping, so unusually quiet it was, licking softly on the stony wall.

Davy had been chosen to speak first and what he had to say was very simple. They must all wait.

"We must all wait on the tide," he said. "It has served us well all our lives and it is the only luck we have."

Harriet looked at the calm sea glinting in the evening sunlight, and found it hard to suspect it of treachery. Her father must be right. But it was clear that many of the villagers disagreed, Horn most of all.

"I say down with shrimps!" he cried. "There's plenty of other fish in the sea, I say!"

A murmur of agreement ran through the crowd.

"There's only shrimps in these parts," said Davy. "Was only shrimps, I mean."

"Then," said Horn, "we must go where there is fish, real fish. I've never thought shrimps was real fish at all come to that."

There was booing then, and cries of "Shame!" The people of Little Shrimpton were proud of their calling and rallied to its defence. Horn held up his hand. His pinkness completed his resemblance to a shrimp.

"Very well," he said, "I will say no more. But I say this. There's been no silver brought to this town for two weeks and more. Five children I have at home to be fed and clothed. Where the silver is, I must go. If there's no silver here – then I shall go!"

There was silence. Horn had spoken

the words that many a man in the crowd was thinking.

"Down the coast!" cried Horn. "That's where the silver is! Silver mackerel and silver herring. There's nets *full* of silver down the coast!"

"Yes, down the coast!" cried the people, fired by the vision of bursting nets and showers of silver. "Down the coast!"

Davy held up his hand for silence and tried to shout above the din, but in vain. Talking excitedly the villagers gathered in groups and made their plans. This man had a horse and cart, this a wagon. They would shut up their houses, take their belongings and go. The Garters, horrified, stared at each other.

"Come along, Fancy and Harriet," said Davy. "Home."

They went in and shut the door. Fancy even banged the shutters to, to muffle the noise and excitement from the quay. They all sat down.

"So it's come to that, has it?" said

Fancy. "Down the coast, is it!"

"Not for us, Fancy," said Davy.

"Shrimps isn't real fish, indeed!" cried Fancy. "And what does Horn know about fish, pray?"

"Are there really other fish down the coast, Mother?" asked Harriet.

"I don't hold with other fish," said Fancy with finality. "I'm a shrimper."

Davy and Harriet may not have found it as easy to keep saying it as Fancy did, but they felt exactly the same. There was really nothing more to be said.

Next morning the whole village was astir. Doors stood wide and furniture and bedding was piled in the streets. Wagons were loaded high with chairs and tables, mattresses and cooking-pots.

"Even the pictures off the walls!" said Fancy in disgust.

The Garters watched all day from their windows.

At noon Horn's family rolled by with four of the children riding on top of a

kitchen table, and the baby in a shrimp
basket.

"First off a sinking ship!" said Fancy
scornfully. "Shrimps isn't real fish indeed!"

It seemed unlikely that she would ever
forgive him this.

As the day wore on, more and more carts passed by the window. At the house opposite Samual Stone began to nail the shutters down – bang, bang, bang – till Fancy covered her ears with her hands and Harriet felt her head begin to ache.

All through the next day the work went on. The men saw their families safely off in the wagons, then took to the water in their boats and made off down the coast. Some of them came in to shake hands and make their farewells, and seeing their downcast eyes Harriet could not find it in her heart to blame them. They did not want to go, any more than the Garters did. They were simply less obstinate.

By the evening of the third day the village was deserted. The last cart rolled past the windows and disappeared into the gathering dusk.
Then there was silence.
The three Garters
opened the door
and ventured out.

There were no lamps behind the windows, no sails to watch for, no eager women on the jetty. Even the tide was out.

"It's quiet," Davy suggested at last.

"Quietish," agreed Fancy.

A last gull called and their eyes followed the white shape into the smudging gloom. Now it seemed they had the whole world to themselves.

"I've just had a fancy!" cried Fancy suddenly, and the others started.

She began to laugh, pushing at her wispy hair with her hands as she always did when she was excited.

"Fancy if you was to go out tomorrow all by yourself, Davy, and if those shrimps was to have come *back*!" Her hands left her hair and flew clear into the air at the thought. "Fancy if they was to be *there*, thick as noodles in a broth! Oh, Davy, fancy!"

Harriet and Davy stood there quietly, trying hard to fancy it. Slowly Fancy's laughter died away.

"Oh well," she said. "Supper, then.
Toasted cheese. That I am sure of.
Drat shrimps!"
The Garters went inside and shut the door.
All the doors in Little Shrimpton were
shut now.

CHAPTER FIVE

A NEW PLAN

A NEW WAY OF LIFE BEGAN FOR THE Garters.

"We've got to learn to live by ourselves," said Fancy. "And that'll mean work, all round."

In the past a cart had come from Lower Herring each week with supplies for the village, with extra dainties and fruit and vegetables.

"And now we shall have to grow our own," said Fancy.

There was a patch of thin, poor soil behind the house and Davy dug it as deep as he was able and sowed potatoes, carrots and beans. The Garters borrowed a cart from a nearby farmer and went into Lower Herring. There they bought sacks of flour, oil for the lamp, and a big salted ham to hang from the ceiling.

"What we really want," said Fancy thoughtfully, "is a cow."

"No room," said Davy, thinking of his newly planted garden.

"Village green," said Fancy.

So a cow they bought, and half a dozen hens, which were to be Harriet's. They trundled home with their laden wagon, feeling like real farmers, singing songs and waving switches they had cut from the hedge.

Only when they drove into the shuttered village, when the wheels stopped rolling and the silence crept up on them again, did their spirits sink. To be sure, the tide flapped idly under the jetty and the gulls wheeled and screamed under the low cliffs just as they always had, but the people were missing, and they had left a silence that all the sea noises in the world could not hide.

They sat there blankly.

"We shall get used to it," said Fancy in the end. "It's not as if anyone *likes* a lot

of noise."

They fetched the cow out of the wagon, and she slid unsteadily over the cobbles. She mooed and roused a storm of indignant echoes that scattered the gulls perched on the nearby roofs. While Davy led her up to the green Fancy and Harriet saw to the hens, and it was dark before the wagon was unloaded and everything stowed and ship-shape.

That night the Garters were too tired
to notice that the stars were the only lights
out over the bay, or to miss the soft,
knocking chorus of fifty boats against the
sea wall.

The days that followed were too full to
leave much time for brooding. Davy gave
up going to sea. Instead, Harriet was sent
down to the sands each morning with her
net to try the pools for shrimps. Davy
tended his garden and fished from the
harbour wall to catch their dinner. Fancy
milked the cow and made butter. She
missed the shrimp-boiling less now that she
had her churning. She could be heard
singing lustily in the little outhouse that
she now called the dairy, and she gloated
over her pale curls of butter almost as
lovingly as she had ladled her rosy shrimps.

At first they all took it for granted that
one day, soon, the shrimps would come
back. But as the weeks passed and each
day, twice a day, the tide came in empty-
handed, hope dwindled. So did the

Garters' savings. Soon the shrimping
season would be over, and the long winter
lay ahead, with only a handful of silver to
see them through.

After she had gone to bed Harriet
would hear Fancy and Davy talking in low
worried voices by the dim light of a lamp
turned low to save the oil.

Then, one morning, she found out
what they had been saying.

"You'll have to go to Aunt Lavinia's,
Harriet," said Fancy. She was in the middle
of making bread and was kneading the
dough hard.

"We've come down to shells," she went
on, "though I never thought to live to see
the day."

"But I live here!" cried Harriet. "I
don't want to live with Aunt Lavinia!"

"I didn't say live with her," said Fancy.
"Just stop with her, and pick up how it's
done. Davy and me have the whole thing
planned. You stop there with Lavinia and
go picking shells – sacks full if you can – to

bring back. Then you can learn a few odd things, such as threading cockles and such, and home you come. That way, we've a second trade to our hands. If we're lucky, shells will see us through the winter."

She waved a triumphant, floury hand and Davy nodded from the corner.

"What about my hens?" cried Harriet, looking for a loop-hole. Aunt Lavinia was old, she went in for smelling salts and herb tea and didn't hold with bare feet.

But Harriet knew that she had to go. If she didn't, then *all* the Garter's would have to go - perhaps for ever. Secretly, she half wanted to go, once she became used to the idea. Whenever she went to Lower Herring she loved to gather shells, enjoying their dry powdery feel and their bleached colours. Besides, Lower Herring was filled with people, doors stood open and there was talk and laughter. Harriet was tired of echoes and the empty streets of Little Shrimpton.

She packed her bag that evening, taking only the dresses without patches and both her pairs of shoes.

Next day, wearing her best blue velvet and two rows of Aunt Lavinia's painted cockles, she went to Lower Herring, seated between Davy and Fancy on the borrowed farmer's cart.

In Aunt Lavinia's tiny parlour, the walls
so thick with shells as to seem barnacled,
Davy and Fancy unfolded their plan. Aunt
Lavinia nodded frequently and, when they
had done, said to Harriet, "Hold out your
hands!"

Puzzled, Harriet spread her fingers.

"Hmmm!" said Aunt Lavinia. "They
might be good shell fingers. We shall have
to see."

Harriet hid her hands behind her skirts
and caught Fancy having a quick look at
her own big red fingers before tucking
them under the edges of her shawl. Davy
did not even bother to look at his, thick
and salt-bitten as they were. He just edged
them slowly into his pockets and refused a
second spiced bun for fear of taking them
out again.

It was agreed that Harriet should stay
for three weeks. "Not that she can hope
for much in *that* time," said Aunt Lavinia.
"Hardly time to learn to thread a cockle,
let alone oil an oyster or tint a limpet.

Sixty years I've been shelling, and even I can sometimes split a scallop or chip a razor clam."

"Oh, not often, Lavinia, I'm sure," murmured Fancy.

And Davy jerked his head towards the encrusted walls and said, "You've a real pretty way with shells, Lavinia, and we're proud to have Harriet learn from you."

"Oh well," said Aunt Lavinia, "I dare say she *will* learn. And I shall be glad of someone to help with the picking. I don't bend as well as I did."

"Oh, she can *bend!*" cried Fancy. "Can't you Harriet?"

So they all parted cheerfully enough, and as it was only for three weeks there seemed no real need for tears. Harriet shed a few all the same, later, in her new bed with giant whelks for bedknobs and a framed sampler at the head, worked in tiny snails and reading, *Shells are the flowers of the sea*.

"And so are shrimps," was Harriet's last waking thought as she pulled the stiff sheets over her ears, and all night long tides full of shrimps bloomed for her in dreams.

CHAPTER SIX

THE SEA PIPER

WHEN HARRIET WOKE THE NEXT day she could not at first think where she was. After a few moments she made out the whitish shapes of the whelk bedknobs, and remembered. It was very quiet. There was none of the banging and clatter that Fancy believed in at crack of dawn. Harriet supposed that there was little point in Aunt Lavinia getting up early, as shells could be glued and painted at any time of day, and picked too, for that matter.

She remembered the sacks she had brought with her to fill with shells and decided to begin straight away. Softly she rose and dressed and tiptoed out, carrying a basket and a pair of shoes. It would never do to come home barefoot. Through the sleeping shell-parlour she stole and out through the back door. A fine white mist blew against her face.

In the distance she could hear the voices of the Lower Herring fishermen as they made their boats ready for the day's sailing. She went in the other direction, out towards the edge of town where she knew that the sands lay mile upon mile, thickly sown with shells for the gathering. Where the sea wall ended she stopped and buried her shoes under a mound of dry sand. Then she ran down into the mist.

Soon she was picking shells in a white and silent world of her own. Even the sound of the sea was stilled and not a gull called from the hidden town. She might have been at the end of nowhere. On she went, stooping, gathering, seeing how the chalky colours of the shells were brought into life by the dew of the mist.

When at last she stopped and straightened up, the mist had begun to lift and was pierced with sun. She saw that she was no longer alone.

The figure she saw might almost have been part of the mist itself, dressed in flowing tatters of grey and blue, thin, spider-legged and swiftly moving. Just then the sun broke through and he stood on stilts of shadow, a sudden giant on the bare shining flats.

Behind her the gulls began to scream above the town and to race out to sea for their first fish. The figure stopped. He raised a pipe to his lips and began to play. The music was thin and sweet, but crowded, so that it seemed not one melody he played but a thousand, all drawn out of

that one slim reed. It had as many voices as the sea itself.

And as he played all the gulls that had flown seaward came winging to him and flew about him, circling and silent. He turned about and stepped away on his steeple legs, still playing, while the gulls followed and Harriet stared herself into a kind of blindness. She did not really see him go at all. One minute he was there, tatters streaming like rags in the mist, the next he was gone. The music had gone too, and the gulls.

Harriet shaded her eyes and looked back towards the town. The empty roofs glittered in the sun. There was not a gull in sight. Only the weathercock, stone-still with his iron wings, was left.

Harriet picked up her basket of shells and ran, pell-mell, back to the town, fumble-footed in the soft sand. Past the sea wall she flew, up the street and into the kitchen of Aunt Lavinia's house.

"Mercy!" shrieked Aunt Lavinia.

"Where are your shoes, girl?"

They were buried down by the sea wall. Harriet stared at her in her cross-stitched apron, with her frilled cap and ringlets carefully edging her ears.

"I don't *hold* with bare feet," said Aunt Lavinia.

Harriet knew then, quite certainly, that whatever it was she had seen Aunt Lavinia would not hold with it. Never in a thousand years would she hold with it. She put her basket of shells on the floor and Aunt Lavinia frowned as little trickles of dry sand ran on to the red tiles.

"I'm sorry," she said. "I *did* take my shoes. But I left them buried down by the sea wall."

"Then *fetch* them!" shrilled Aunt Lavinia. "Fetch them before the sand gets into the leather!"

Harriet fled.

For the rest of the day she did not leave the house. She dutifully dusted the shells in the parlour and learned how to make glue.

She watched Aunt Lavinia turn mussel shells into butter dishes.

But in the evening, after supper, Aunt Lavinia put on her lace mittens, sat in her rocking chair and nodded off. For the second time that day Harriet stole away and walked the deserted streets of Lower Herring, looking for a gull. The chimney-pots were empty. She *must* have seen what she had seen.

She went back and sorted her shells, waiting for Aunt Lavinia to wake up and go to bed. All the while she thought of the piper leading a ribbon of gulls into nowhere, and wondered.

CHAPTER SEVEN

MATTHEW'S TALE

NEXT DAY THE PEOPLE OF LOWER
Herring began to notice that the
gulls were missing. Harriet went
down to the market to fetch a crab for
dinner, and everywhere was talk and
excitement. To Harriet, who knew exactly
what was happening to the gulls, it was
odd to hear them guessing.

It was odd, too, to see so many of her

old friends from Lower Shrimpton. They greeted her kindly and asked after Davy and Fancy, but they did not seem happy. "No sign of the shrimps yet?" they asked wistfully, and Harriet knew that at the first sign of a shrimp's whisker in Shrimpton Bay they would be back up on their wagons and bowling helter-skelter back up the coast to home.

Horn she found glumly tarring beams by the pier. There was no carrying for him now, and his horse and cart stood idly by. The hands that had counted silver daily were blackened with pitch, and Harriet wondered if now perhaps he thought shrimps *might* be real fish after all.

The real excitement of the day came in the evening, when the Lower Herring fleet sailed in. A meeting was held in the square to deal with the matter of the missing seagulls. Aunt Lavinia would not go herself for fear of being jostled, but she sent Harriet, bidding her mark well everything that was said.

In the square the Mayor was standing on the stone steps of the market cross, and by his side was a grey-bearded fisherman, bent and leaning on a stick.

"The gulls have flown," announced the Mayor, waving a pudgy hand towards the sky. "The shrimps have gone from Little Shrimpton. There's the oddest things going on along this coast, and no one to tell the why or wherefore. It's my opinion that it's the weather that's to blame."

The crowd muttered and peered up at the sky, looking for signs.

"Old Matthew here," went on the Mayor, "thinks *he* knows the answer. I have decided to let him speak."

The people cheered. Matthew raised his knobbed stick and silence fell.

"It's my belief," he said, "that all of this is the work of the Sea Piper."

At his words the hush deepened, not a stir or sound came from the listening people.

"You'll have heard of him, maybe," Matthew went on. "You'll have heard tales of him at your mother's knee, how he's the brother of the Pied Piper that brought the rats out of Hamelin and led the children into the mountain. The Sea Piper can lead every living creature of the sea by the notes of his magic pipe. He comes and goes and never a human soul sets eyes on him."

The Mayor coughed and fidgeted with his chain, but every face in the crowd was turned on the wrinkled leather-faced fisherman.

"Only a child may see him," said Matthew, "and that rarely, once or twice in a hundred years. *I* saw him, eighty years ago and more, and never a word of it have I said until this day."

A soft gasp ran about the square and ebbed away.

"I saw him on yon very beach," said Matthew, "piping sea-gulls to him in a mist. I asked him why he stole our gulls, and he said, for loneliness. 'I pipe alone with my own shadow', says he. 'Always alone. That is why I take the gulls. But I shall bring them back before long'.

And sure enough he did, that very night. Out of the whole town there was only me to know they had gone at all. They came at sunset."

He looked beyond to the darkening sky over the sea. "At about the time of day it is now. I saw them fly back over the chimney-pots and ran down that road, down that beach, as fast as the wind. But he was gone."

Harriet, her heart thudding, looked up at the empty chimney-pots and the silvery streaked sky, and all in a moment knew what she must do. No one saw her leave the square or heard her flying footsteps over the cobbled road down to the sea.

As she started down the long empty beach, away from the town, beyond the gasping of her own breath Harriet thought she heard the sea-gulls. She stopped for a minute, listening. Very faint and far away she heard them, and though she strained her eyes into the gloom she could see no sign of them. She saw only the faint fringe of sea glowing in the darkness, and the last silvery shreds of daylight in the sky.

She ran along the firmer sand newly left by the tide. The wet sand closed her footprints behind her. She left no trace. And all the while the crying of the gulls grew louder until suddenly they went over in a train of white. Their crying deafened her and she did not hear the Sea Piper's music until she saw him, face to face.

She stopped. He stood a little way from her, still piping. His tatters seemed one with the darkness as they had with the mist, and she could make out only the pale shape of his face. The gulls' cries faded, the music died away and he took the pipe from his lips. He did not speak, and for fear that he had not seen her and would be gone in an instant with his quick light strides as he had that morning, Harriet called softly, "Sea Piper! Sea Piper!"

He nodded slowly.

"Sea Piper, help us, please!"

She thought he bent his head as if
ready to listen, and she poured out the
story of how first the shrimps had gone
from Little Shrimpton, and now the people
themselves, leaving only the Garters and
their echoes. She told how the weeds were
growing between the stones and the birds
nesting in the deserted houses.

"And soon *we* shall have to go, too!" she cried desperately. "We can't stay for ever without shrimps, even *Fancy* says that!"

The Sea Piper was slowly nodding and Harriet thought that he smiled.

"And, Sea Piper," she said then, remembering old Matthew's words, "we will make you a gift in return. You shall have all the gulls of Little Shrimpton, every one of them. You shall pipe them away and keep them for ever, for company on your journeys."

She stood silent. In the distance came voices and shouting. The people of Lower Herring had seen the gulls fly home and were hurrying to the beach in the hope of a glimpse of the Sea Piper.

"Oh, quickly, quickly!" cried Harriet. "Please give me your answer."

He nodded suddenly. "I will do it," he said, "and now listen, what you must do."

Harriet listened eagerly while all the time the shouting grew louder, and just as

the light of torches fell on to them and the
Sea Piper's shadow sprang to a steeple
again, he had done and was gone.

The dark swallowed him at a single
gulp as the mist had done.

Harriet turned to face the bobbing
army of torches, blinking at the dazzle.

"Why, it's Harriet Garter!" she heard the Shrimpton people cry, and "Who is it? Who is it?" from the Lower Herring folk, who did not know her face.

"Have you seen him? Did you see him?" the cry went up from them all alike, and Harriet smiled.

"I have seen him and I have spoken with him," she replied, "and I asked him a favour, which he has granted. All the people of Little Shrimpton must be home by tomorrow night, because, the day after, the men will have to be up early. The shrimps will be back in the bay."

There was a moment's silence and then a roar went up, rocking the torchlight and sending shadows swinging far out over the sands.

All of a sudden Harriet found herself being lifted and carried shoulder high, with the heads of the procession bobbing below her. The noise and light left the beach and went up into the town.

Only the Sea Piper walked the shore

alone, hugging the promise of a hundred gulls and the end of silence.

CHAPTER EIGHT

PIPING UP THE SHRIMPS

A T DAWN NEXT DAY HARRIET WAS packing her bag while Aunt Lavinia slumbered on, worn out by the goings-on of the night before. When Harriet had been borne home by the excited townspeople, treading on her garden and waving torches in her dazzled eyes, Aunt Lavinia had needed her smelling salts immediately. When she came round after the first sniff to see so many faces bending over her she had gone straight off again, and Harriet felt obliged to show the visitors out.

Aunt Lavinia had not believed a word of the story about the Sea Piper and was inclined to think that the gulls had not really disappeared at all. As for the rest of it, it was simply a trick of Harriet's to get herself home again.

"*I* never heard of shrimps dancing along to pipes," she said. "Nobody *I* ever knew played tunes for the fishes."

"Of course not!" cried Harriet. "But this is magic!"

"I don't *hold* with magic," retorted Aunt Lavinia, and went to bed.

Harriet knew it was unlikely that Aunt Lavinia had changed in the night and would wake up believing in magic with all her heart, so she tiptoed out as she had done that first morning, barefoot and carrying her bag. The sack of shells she left behind with a little paper saying goodbye and thankyou. Aunt Lavinia had meant no harm. She simply could not help being Aunt Lavinia.

The Little Shrimpton folk were already gathering in the square. They had worked through the night so as to be ready for the journey home. And the rattling of the wagons and their hoarse, excited talk woke the rest of the town, so that soon the streets were as crowded as if it were noon and not still starlight – except at the very eastern edge of the sky.

By the time the whole procession had gathered and the first carts began to trundle out of the square, it was daylight. Harriet, perched on a wagon with a friendly shrimper and his family, almost choked with excitement. And when at last in the afternoon the cart began the long roll down the hill into Little Shrimpton itself, and Harriet saw Davy and Fancy come running out to stare huge-eyed at the advancing wagons, she burst into tears, as she had been tempted to do for most of the day.

Then it was all cheering and shouting, shaking of hands, clapping of backs, and such joy on the faces of Fancy and Davy that you would have thought the heavens had opened and begun to *rain* shrimps.

All Harriet could say was, "The shrimps are coming back! The shrimps are coming back!" And it was only later, when they were inside and Harriet was sitting on the new chair Davy had carved for her, that she told them the whole story.

This time she had a real audience for her tale. There were plenty of things that Fancy herself did not hold with, but magic was definitely not one of them. She gasped and exclaimed extravagantly all through the telling, and at the end said, "Well ! The *Sea Piper*!" Would he come in and have a bite of supper, after, do you think?"

Then Harriet told them what the Sea Piper had made her promise. At sunset, the moment the first star appeared, everyone in Little Shrimpton was to go inside and close the doors and shutters. If so much as a chink showed behind a curtain, he would not keep his promise. No one, not even Harriet herself, was to set eyes on him while the spell was worked.

Fancy was thoroughly disappointed.

"And from what you say, Harriet, he could have done with a good meal," she said wistfully. And Davy added, "I should like to shake him by the hand, and so, I dare say, would every man in Little Shrimpton."

The day passed quickly. Doors and windows were thrown wide, mats were beaten and dusk flew in clouds. By the time evening came every family in Shrimpton was sitting down to supper in its own home, and the Garters themselves felt that theirs was a real home once more, now that the people were back.

"I dare say we shall miss the gulls a bit at first," said Fancy, "but not so much as we missed people. Oh no! And I don't begrudge that poor Piper his bit of company, either."

As the sun began to set a wind blew up from the sea, rattling the doors and windows as if to remind the villagers of their part of the bargain. And so, one by one, with a last look at the sky and the sea, each family went indoors.

One by one the shutters came across and very soon the Garters were in a street as dark and silent as it had been for the past months, only this time there was a difference. They knew that the lamps were burning, even if they were not seen, and the voices there, even though they could not be heard.

The wind blew stronger with every moment, tossing Harriet's skirts about her knees and sending Fancy's hands flying to her hair.

"Come along now," said Davy. "Inside."

He guessed that the two of them were loitering, half hoping for a glimpse of the Piper, despite everything.

"A promise is a promise, Fancy and Harriet," he said.

As they turned to come in, the gulls that had been settling to roost on the roofs and chimney-pots suddenly flew up and began to scream anew, riding on the wind, treading the great gusts as if they were waves at sea.

"He's coming!" shrieked Fancy, suddenly overcome by the thought of magic about to happen on her doorstep. Next minute the Garters were inside and the doors and shutters banged shut.

They waited then, and listened.

At first they heard only the wind, thundering and buffeting about the walls until the little house trembled and the oil-lamps flickered in the cross-draughts. Above the wind they heard the endless crying of the gulls and at last, thin and high, threading the tumult as clearly as a bell, the music of the Sea Piper.

The Garters sat heads cocked, spell-bound.

"Is he calling the shrimps, d'you think, or the sea-gulls?" whispered Fancy.

"The shrimps," said Harriet softly.
She could see them in her mind's
eye, wreathing the bay in their shadowy
thousands, pulled by the notes promising
whatever delights a shrimp dreams of,
longs for in its shrimpmost heart.

For a moment the piping stopped. Then came a new music, one that Harriet half-remembered. The gulls renewed their screaming, and she pictured the Sea Piper striding off now with his catch of white birds, tatters flowing like water behind him in the wind, long legs stepping lightly into nowhere.

The music grew fainter, the last gulls' cries were drowned in the wind. Last of all, the wind dropped, the wooden house steadied itself and stood firm again. The Sea Piper had passed.

Fancy drew a vast, shuddering sigh that was like the last breath of the wind itself.

"Oh, Davy!" she said softly. "Oh Harriet! It was magic! Perfect magic!"

The others nodded slowly.

"And now," she said, with some of her old briskness, "what about your oilskins for the morning, Davy? And where did you leave your net, Harriet? You'll be shrimping tomorrow, I'll be bound."

And so she was. At first light Harriet

was running down the puddled sands, woken by her own excitement, for there was not a gull left in sight. As she reached her first pool she stopped only for a moment to wave an arm to Davy, outward bound.

Then she looked down into the clear depths to see shrimps at last and, for a brief moment before she broke the water with her net, a ragged shape that might have been the reflection of a cloud – or of the Sea Piper?

Another Story Book from Hodder Children's Books

THE LITTLE SEA HORSE

Helen Cresswell

Out of the sea comes an enchanted creature –
a tiny horse of purest white with hooves of
brightest gold.

Molly knows he is far too precious to keep, but
the local townspeople lock the magical horse in
a cage, and throw away the key. Only Molly can
find a way to release him back to the sea.

A lyrical and deeply evocative tale from a
magical storyteller.

Another Story Book from Hodder Children's Books

HAMISH

W. J. Corbett

Hamish is a mountain goat.

All his friends are mountain goats.

The only trouble is – Hamish is terrified of climbing mountains.

Every day his friends clatter off to seek adventure in the high hills, and every day Hamish makes more and more excuses to stay behind in the comfort of his heathery bed.

Until one day, Hamish hears a cry for help – and only he can save the day . . .

ORDER FORM

0 340 63461 8   THE LITTLE SEA HORSE   £2.99
                 Helen Creswell

0 340 61954 6   HAMISH   £2.99
                 W.J. Corbett

All Hodder Children's books are available at your local bookshop or newsagent, or can be ordered direct from the publisher. Just tick the titles you want and fill in the form below. Prices and availability subject to change without notice.

Hodder Children's Books, Cash Sales Department, Bookpoint, 39 Milton Park, Abingdon, OXON, OX14 4TD, UK. If you have a credit card you may order by telephone – (01235) 831700.

Please enclose a cheque or postal order made payable to Bookpoint Ltd to the value of the cover price and allow the following for postage and packing: UK & BFPO – £1.00 for the first book, 50p for the second book, and 30p for each additional book ordered up to a maximum charge of £3.00. OVERSEAS & EIRE – £2.00 for the first book, £1.00 for the second book, and 50p for each additional book.

Name ....

Address...
....
....

If you would prefer to pay by credit card, please complete:

Please debit my Visa/ Access/ Diner's Club/ American Express (delete as applicable) card no:

Signature ....

Expiry Date..